THE GOLDEN COMPASS

™

MOVIE STORYBOOK

KAY WOODWARD

■SCHOLASTIC

Scholastic Children's Books
Euston House, 24 Eversholt Street,
London NW1 1DB, UK
A division of Scholastic Ltd
London – New York – Toronto – Sydney – Auckland
Mexico City – New Delhi – Hong Kong

First published in the UK by Scholastic Ltd, 2007

Editorial Director: Lisa Edwards
Project Manager: Neil Kelly
Project Editor: Laura Milne
Designer: Aja Bongiorno

Adapted from *The Golden Compass*™ movie screenplay by Kay Woodward

ISBN-10: 1 407 10620 1
ISBN-13: 978 1 407 10620 5

2 4 6 8 10 9 7 5 3 1

Papers used by Scholastic Children's Books are made
from wood grown in sustainable forests.

www.scholastic.co.uk

Twelve-year-old Lyra Belacqua lives in the city of Oxford, in the country of Brytain. But it is not the Oxford that we know – Lyra's city is in a world much like our own but in a different universe. Here, each person has a dæmon – a part of their soul that lives outside their body in the form of an animal. A child's dæmon can change shape, but grown-ups' dæmons are settled in one form. Lyra's dæmon is called Pantalaimon, or Pan for short. In the blink of an eye he can change into different animals, such as a cat, an ermine or even a bird.

Lyra is an orphan, and Jordan College in Oxford is the only home she has ever known. Here, she is cared for by the college staff and watched over by Lord Asriel, her wise, fierce uncle. Unfortunately, he is rarely there to make her days more interesting. And when Lyra gets bored she gets into trouble...

One morning, Lyra decided that she and Pan should go exploring.

"Stop clomping about or we'll get caught for sure!" hissed Pan. They were in the Dining Hall of Jordan College. The little dæmon sat on Lyra's shoulder, bristling with annoyance. "See if there's anybody in the corridor," she said, peering from the shadows where they hid.

Obediently, Pan changed into a bird. He fluttered to a door and looked around it. The coast was clear. At once, he and Lyra headed to the Retiring Room – a large, comfortable chamber where the Master and Scholars of Jordan met to talk.

"There, we've seen it now," said Pantalaimon nervously. "Happy?"

"No, I want to look around," said Lyra. She went over to the big meeting table and pinged a crystal glass with her fingernail.

"You do know that if you get a spanking, I hurt too?" Pan spoke the truth – humans and their dæmons shared an invisible bond. Whatever a human felt, so did their dæmon.

"What d'you think they talk about in here?" said Lyra, ignoring him.

There wasn't time to find out. Suddenly they heard the sound of voices in the corridor outside.

Looking around, Lyra saw a huge wardrobe in the corner of the room. Quickly, they dived inside. Lyra pulled the wardrobe door until it was almost shut and peeked through the narrow gap.

The Master of Jordan College walked into the room. A sinister-looking man accompanied him.

"As Master of Jordan, you must force Lord Asriel to abandon his plans," said the man. His name was Fra Pavel, an important person from the Magisterium – the authority that ruled Lyra's world.

The Master looked displeased. "His proposal will be heard," he said, then left the room.

Fra Pavel took a packet from his pocket and poured the white, powdery contents into a bottle of wine. Then, he too was gone.

Moments later, Lord Asriel appeared in the doorway of the Retiring Room with his snow-leopard dæmon, Stelmaria. He poured himself a glass of wine. Lyra burst out of the wardrobe and knocked the glass from his hand.

"It's poisoned!" she cried. "I saw that man from the Magisterium do it."

Asriel frowned and looked closely at the bottle. Then, at the sound of footsteps, he gestured towards the wardrobe. "Back in there with you, quick," he said. Lyra and Pan obeyed.

"Lord Asriel," said the Master as he came in with a group of scholars. "May I introduce Fra Pavel?"

"I've followed your exploits closely," said Fra Pavel. His eyes narrowed as he saw the broken wine glass.

Asriel switched on a projector, which beamed a three-dimensional picture on to the wall. It showed a man and his dæmon standing on ice. Glittering, dust-like particles streamed from the sky to the man's body.

"I took this photogram at the magnetic North Pole, in Svalbard, the kingdom of the Ice Bears," said Asriel. "As you see, Dust is flowing into the man through his dæmon." There were gasps of astonishment from the Jordan College scholars.

"What is that?" asked the Master, pointing at the picture. Lyra squinted at the image. The sky was filled with swirling, glowing streams of light. But behind the light there appeared to be a city – with towers, domes, walls and streets – hanging in the air!

"It is a city in another world" said Asriel.

"From there, and from a billion other worlds, Dust flows."

"Lies..." breathed Fra Pavel.

"That is the truth," said Asriel. "To find the source of Dust, I intend to travel to those other worlds. I humbly beg the college council to fund such a journey."

Later that day, Lyra and her friend Roger Parslow lay talking on the college roof. Roger, a Jordan College servant boy, listened patiently as Lyra told him about her experience in the Retiring Room.

"Asriel said he'd take me to the North," Lyra lied. Her uncle had done nothing of the sort. He'd left that morning – after receiving his money and warning Lyra to behave.

"I'm supposed to keep an eye on them Gobblers. They took them Gyptian kids up Banbury way. Billy Costa told me."

The Gyptians were rough, tough traders who travelled by water. Many Gyptian children had disappeared recently – the "Gobblers" was the name people had given to the kidnappers.

"I heard them Gobblers take you down to Hell," said Roger, grimly.

"You're afraid of them, aren't you?" asked Lyra. "Roger, I promise – if you was taken by the Gobblers, I would come and rescue you," she said. "You'd come to get me too, wouldn't you?"

"Course," said Roger. "But everybody would go looking for you. I'm just a servant. You're a lady."

Lyra was furious. She wasn't a lady! Fuming, she went off for dinner. Left alone, Roger wandered around the college grounds.

He heard an odd, piping whistle.

"Lyra? Is that you?" he asked. The only reply was a rustle in the undergrowth. A monkey, with sleek, golden fur and intelligent eyes, suddenly appeared.

"Who are you?" said Roger. His dæmon, in the shape of a butterfly, fluttered over to the creature. The Golden Monkey smiled – and trapped the butterfly in its paw. Now Roger was really scared.

"Let her go!" he cried. He looked up and spotted someone else. "Let us go!"

Scrubbed, clean and very grumpy, Lyra sat among the male scholars at the dining table, feeling outnumbered. Then she blinked. A woman had arrived – a beautiful, glamorous woman wearing a dazzling smile.

"Who's she?" muttered Pan.

The Master answered. "Lyra, this is Mrs Coulter."

Lyra thought Mrs Coulter was wonderful. She was clever and knowledgable, and she knew Lyra's Uncle Asriel. But when Lyra found out that Mrs Coulter had also met the king of the Ice Bears, her admiration shot through the roof.

Mrs Coulter even told her a secret. "King Ragnar is desperate to have a dæmon of his own," she whispered. "Bears don't have them, you see."

Lyra nodded, speechless with wonder.

"I'm going back to the North soon," said Mrs Coulter. "Perhaps you should come along."

"Me?" Lyra gasped. Mrs Coulter smiled. "I had better get the Master's permission."

The Master looked rather scared by the question. And he seemed sure that Asriel would not agree.

"Lyra ... do you wish to go?" he asked.

"Yes, please!" she exclaimed. Mrs Coulter's dæmon stroked Pan.

It was a monkey, with beautiful, golden fur...

The next morning, the Master visited Lyra. He was carrying a leather satchel, from which he produced a golden object. It looked very much like a compass.

"It is an alethiometer," said the Master. "It was given to the college by Lord Asriel. And now I am giving it to you."

"But what's it for?" asked Lyra.

The Master's reply was solemn. "It tells the truth. And it is very important that Mrs Coulter does not know you have it."

The hours flew by until Lyra was ready to leave Oxford. But Roger had not come to say goodbye and Mrs Coulter would not wait for him.

Puzzled by Mrs Coulter's impatience and irritation, Lyra followed her to the waiting sky ferry.

It was a wonderful journey. The vast city of London sprawled beneath them, full of amazing buildings and landmarks. At its centre was the great Magisterium building.

When they landed, they were whisked away to Mrs Coulter's house, which was beautiful, just like her. Lyra even had her own pretty, pink-and-white room.

As soon as she and Pan were alone, they looked at the alethiometer. Around the edge of its face, there were symbols. It had hands, like a clock, turned by special knobs, and a slowly spinning needle.

"The Master said it told the truth," whispered Pan.

"Ask it something."

Lyra spoke clearly.

"What's Dust?"

She'd longed to find out, ever since Asriel had spoken of it.

But the needle just swung round and round.

There was a gentle knock and Lyra had just enough time to hide the alethiometer under her pillow before the door opened. It was Mrs Coulter, come to tuck Lyra in. "Sleep well – we've got a busy day tomorrow," she said, putting out the light. As the bedroom door closed again, Lyra heard the Golden Monkey chittering.

"He was looking at the pillow," whispered Pan. Lyra felt a sudden chill. Quickly, her hand closed around the alethiometer. Maybe the Master had been right to warn her about Mrs Coulter...

The next few days were a whirlwind of excitement. Mrs Coulter took Lyra shopping and out to dinner. They were pampered at the beauty parlour. Everything was new and amazing. But Pan wasn't happy.

"She's never going to the North," he grumbled one evening after yet another dinner. "She's going to keep you here for ever." Lyra was speechless with surprise.

On one occasion, Lyra decided to try and impress Mrs Coulter by talking about Dust. But Mrs Coulter's reaction was not what she expected.

"A wise person," said Mrs Coulter, her voice low and dangerous, "knows that there are some things we don't speak about ... Now, will you please take off that childish bag and put it away?"

Lyra looked at the satchel. The alethiometer was hidden inside it.

"No," she said.

"If you do not obey me," hissed Mrs Coulter, "we will have an argument, which I will win." She caught Lyra's wrist as the Golden Monkey grabbed Pan's neck and dragged him away from Lyra.

"Stop pulling us apart!" cried Lyra. "It hurts!"

"Do as I tell you, then," said Mrs Coulter.

Lyra had no choice but to obey. But she had grown suspicious. Something wasn't right. Later that evening, she and Pan explored the house. They weren't sure what they would discover. But in Mrs Coulter's study, they found more than they had bargained for.

"Look!" said Pan.

It was a list of names and strange words, including "Dust Count: 0.0013", "Intercision", and "General Oblation Board."

"What's the General Oblation Board?" Lyra muttered. Pan spelt out the initials. "G, O, B..."

"Gobblers!" gasped Lyra in disbelief.

"She's running the Gobblers!" They sped back to Lyra's room, where she had left her satchel. But the Golden Monkey had beaten them to it and he had the alethiometer!

"No!" cried Lyra.

Pan changed into a bird, plucked the golden object from the Monkey's paw and flew out of the window. Lyra jumped after him.

That night, London was crawling with Magisterial police. Lyra and Pan stuck to the safety of the shadows, trying to keep themselves out of sight.

Searching for somewhere safe to sleep, Lyra and Pan didn't realise that they were being followed. Without warning, a net was thrown over them. But then a shower of arrows fell on their captors. "Gyptians!" exclaimed Lyra, seeing their rescuers. A fierce-looking woman stepped forward. Lyra recognised her at once – it was Ma Costa, the mother of Billy Costa, her friend in Oxford. Ma Costa explained that the Gyptians had been watching over Lyra ever since she left Jordan College. "You're safe with us," she said.

Lyra and Pan were taken by barge to the *Noorderlicht*, a large ship waiting on the open sea. There, they met John Faa – the king of the Gyptians – and Farder Coram, a wise Gyptian elder. They were so kind to her that Lyra showed them the alethiometer.

John Faa had a question for the device.

"We want to know if our spies are well," he said.

Lyra concentrated hard. The alethiometer's needle spun around. But it kept coming back to the hourglass and skull – the symbol of death and disaster.

"I pray you read it wrong," said John Faa. Ma Costa told Lyra that her son Billy had been kidnapped – and then John Faa revealed that Lyra's friend, Roger, had also been captured.

The Gobblers had taken them to the North, along with many other children. The Gyptians' minds were made up – they were going to rescue them all!

Before long, a badly injured spy arrived. He and two fellow spies had discovered that the Gobblers were receiving their orders from the Magisterium. The other spies had been killed or captured, and he was dying – just as the alethiometer had told Lyra. Suddenly, two buzzing black shapes flew on to the ship's deck. They were spy-flies, clockwork creatures used by the Magisterium to track its enemies. One was imprisoned in a strong tin, but the other escaped before it could be caught.

It was a long journey to the North, over rough seas. One night, Lyra stood at the ship's rail. A dark figure swooped out of the sky and landed on the deck.

Lyra turned slowly to see a young, beautiful woman.

"Who are you?" she breathed.

"My name is Serafina Pekkala," was the reply. "I am Clan-Queen of the Witches of Lake Enara.

"A witch…" whispered Lyra.

"Farder Coram wishes to know where the Gobblers take their prey," said Serafina. It is a place called the Experimental Station. The witches call it Bolvangar."

Then she disappeared into the starry night.

$\mathcal{D}$ays later, they arrived at the northern port of Trollesund. Lyra sat near the bustling dock, studying the alethiometer. She was still amazed by her natural ability to read the device. A tall man with long, white hair came over and introduced himself.

"Lee Scoresby," he said. "And this old girl is Hester." He pointed to his hare dæmon. "If I was on the sorta … scout I reckon you're on, I'd hire me an aeronaut," he said, pointing to himself. "And an armoured bear."

"An armoured bear!" said Lyra in amazement.

"There's one in town," said Lee Scoresby. "Iorek Byrnison's his name." Then he raised his hat and walked off. Lyra told Farder Coram what she'd learnt. Together, they went looking for the bear and found him working in a scrapyard. He was a dirty-white colour, unfriendly and very, very big.

"Why are you wasting your time here?" asked Lyra.

Iorek explained that he had been exiled from Svalbard, and that the people of Trollesund had taken his armour away. Lyra quickly asked the alethiometer where Iorek's armour was being kept. "Your armour is in the district office of the Magisterium," she said. With a mighty roar, Iorek burst into action, heading for the town as fast as his huge legs could carry him.

When he reached the offices, Iorek smashed down the doors with a single mighty blow. Within moments he had found his precious armour. As he emerged into the street, a squad of armed police raised their rifles, ready to fire. But the sudden appearance of Lee Scoresby, Lyra and the Gyptians prevented any further trouble, and Iorek was soon allowed to go on his way.

A few short hours later, the Ice Bear and Lee Scoresby had both agreed to join the Gyptians on their mission. So they all left town, wearing their warmest clothes and dragging sledges behind them. Lee Scoresby's airship was in pieces, carefully stored on more sledges. As they trudged on, the weather grew colder. Soon, the ground was covered with snow. Lyra walked beside her new friend, Iorek Byrnison.

"The alethiometer keeps telling me something," she said. "In the next valley, there's a lake with a hut by it. It's something to do with the Gobblers, and Roger... Could you take me there?"

That night, the Ice Bear covered the snowy ground quickly with large strides. Lyra hung on to his warm fur. Iorek slowed to a walk as they approached the frozen lake. On its shores was a hut.

Lyra pushed open the door of the hut. In the dim light, she saw a young boy – *without* a dæmon! How could this be? All humans had dæmons!

"Ratter?" said the boy. Suddenly Lyra realised who he was. It was Billy Costa – Ratter was the name of his missing dæmon.

"Billy?" said Lyra gently. "It's Lyra, from Oxford. Let me take you to your mum."

It didn't take long for Lyra and Billy to get back to the camp. "My son!" cried Ma Costa. She ran over to him and hugged him, sobbing.

Suddenly, there was a whistling sound, then shouts and gunshots. The camp was being attacked!

As the Gyptians fought back, Lyra was captured by one of the attackers. Within moments, she was tied up and thrown on to a sledge. Quickly, it sped away.

The kidnappers took Lyra and Pan far across the ice to a strange, white building. This must be Bolvangar, thought Lyra – the place that the witch Serafina Pekkala had warned them about. The Gobblers brought the children that they kidnapped to Bolvangar. And now she and Pan were about to join the Gobblers' victims!

A man greeted them at the door of the building.

"What's your name?" he asked.

"Lizzie Brooks," lied Lyra. The agents of the Magisterium were after her – she had to keep her real name secret in case this man worked for them.

Lyra was taken through endless white corridors.

"What do you do here?" Lyra asked.

"We help children grow up," said the man. Suddenly, a bell clanged loudly. "I'm afraid we'll have to finish our chat later," he said. "You'd better run along to dinner."

The man showed Lyra into a big, bright and colourful canteen. Children were everywhere, but in the sea of faces, Lyra saw only one. Roger!

He was overjoyed to see her.

"I knew you'd come!," he said. "I promised, didn't I?" she replied. Lyra smiled at her friend.

"Do you know what they do to the kids here?"

"They say they're gonna do this operation," Roger replied. "Then they'll send us home and we won't have to worry about Dust … but once they call a kid in for the operation, you never see them again. They took Billy Costa away last week, and he's still gone."

Lyra gulped. "We've come to rescue you – me and the Gyptians," she said. "Tell the kids to have their warm clothes ready."

"When?" Roger asked eagerly.

"That's what I need to find out…" said Lyra. "But not here. I need to be alone."

Looking around carefully to make sure they weren't being watched, Roger led Lyra out of the canteen. He showed her to a small, unoccupied dining room.

"Be quick," he said. Lyra slipped inside, leaving Roger outside in the corridor. She asked the alethiometer when the Gyptians were coming. "It won't answer!" she whispered to Pan. "But it says I mustn't let Mrs Coulter get hold of it or—" She stopped as footsteps sounded in the corridor.

"I'm very interested in discovering just how children wandered free from the station," said a voice.

It was Mrs Coulter!

Lyra and Pan dived under the dining room table, just as Mrs Coulter and a group of Bolvangar staff came into the room.

"But enough of that for now," Lyra heard Mrs Coulter say. "I have good news. Lord Asriel is imprisoned in Svalbard by the king of the bears."

Lyra gasped in horror.

"Now… it's been a long journey. I think I'll go to bed," said Mrs Coulter. With that, she left the room.

Lyra shuddered, scraping the table accidentally.

"What was that noise?" asked a male voice. Before Lyra knew what was happening, the Bolvangar staff had found her hiding place. Seconds later they were pulling her out from under the table.

They marched her to a room filled with humming, shiny machinery. In the centre of the room there was a device that looked like a cage divided into two compartments.

Lyra struggled as the staff put her in one compartment and Pan in the other.

"This is how you grow up," said a man in a white coat.

A shiny, glowing blade descended towards Lyra and Pan. They were going to cut the invisible bond of energy that connected Lyra and her dæmon!

"Lyra!" cried a woman's voice.

The world span, and Lyra passed out.

Lyra awoke sometime later in Mrs Coulter's chambers. It was her voice she had heard!

"No one's going to harm you, darling," Mrs Coulter said gently. "You don't have to go back with the other children."

"But why do you do it to them?" asked Lyra.

"It's for their own good," said Mrs Coulter. "Just a little cut and they're safe from Dust for ever."

"What's so bad about Dust?" said Lyra.

"Dust is evil itself," said Mrs Coulter. "When you are old enough for your dæmon to settle, Dust gets into you through your dæmon. But all it takes to stop it from happening is a snip. Your dæmon doesn't die – he's just not connected."

"Then why didn't you let them do it to me?"

Mrs Coulter took a deep breath.

"Because I'm your mother."

Lyra felt sick. Then she realized something that she'd known deep down all along.

"Lord Asriel is my father, isn't he?"

Mrs Coulter nodded. Then she smiled and said, "I almost forgot. The Master of Jordan gave you an alethiometer, didn't he?"

Lyra knew what to do. "Here it is," she said, handing Mrs Coulter the tin containing the captured spy-fly. She loosened the lid, and the buzzing, angry creature flew out of the tin. Mrs Coulter screamed as Lyra and Pan ran from the room.

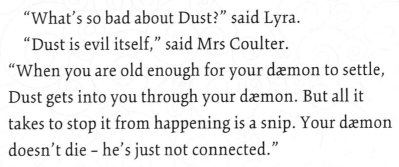

"Come on!" shouted Lyra, when she found Roger and the other children. She led the way to the exit. They burst through the door into the freezing night. But when the children saw the fierce guards and their wolf dæmons, they hung back. The guards attacked.

A dæmon hurled itself at Lyra, but it was batted out of the air by a huge Ice Bear paw. "Iorek!" cried Lyra.

The witches – led by Serafina Pekkala – had come too. They flew through the air, raining arrows on the guards. One witch landed beside Lyra.

"Lead the children away," said Serafina Pekkala. "My sisters will hold off the guards."

Lyra nodded and urged the children on. Then the Gyptians appeared, swiftly followed by Lee Scoresby in his airship.

"Miss Lyra!" he cried. "You wanted to fly, didn't you?" With Iorek, Lyra, Pan and Roger on board, the aeronaut took off into the night sky. He set course for Svalbard, where Lord Asriel was being held captive.

Later, the wind grew stronger. Snow whirled all around. There was a monstrous crash and the airship tilted. Lyra and Pan found themselves falling through the air. They landed in a thick snowdrift. Then two shapes loomed out of the blizzard – Svalbard Ice Bears, from the palace of King Ragnar.

"Come with us," one said. "You are a prisoner."

At the palace, Lyra saw that Ragnar was even bigger than Iorek. She knew that Iorek would be looking for her. But Ragnar would have him killed before he even got through the palace gates!

In a flash, she remembered Mrs Coulter's words. The king of the Ice Bears wanted a dæmon.

"Pan!" she whispered. "I need you to hide."

Pan didn't need to be told twice.

"I am Iorek Byrnison's dæmon!" said Lyra.

Suddenly, she had the bear-king's attention.

"I'd rather belong to you," she continued. "If you defeat him in single combat, great king, I will become your dæmon."

Ragnar smiled. He had exiled Iorek from Svalbard – now he would take his dæmon, too!

I orek arrived at Svalbard the next day, with Roger on his back. To his surprise, he was allowed near the front of the palace. When Lyra told him about her plan he was very pleased.

"I shall call you Lyra Silvertongue," he said proudly.

And so the battle began. It was fierce, loud and bloody. The two Ice Bears punched, slashed, screamed and roared. Ragnar was winning. Injured, Iorek limped away into a corner. Ragnar moved in for the kill, but the battle was not over yet. With one final, mighty blow, Iorek finished it. Ragnar lay dead.

"Who is your king?" Iorek bellowed to all the Svalbard bears.

"Iorek Byrnison!" they cried.

That night, Roger and Lyra explored Ragnar's palace together. They soon found Asriel's rooms. "Uncle Asriel," she said. "Father?"

Asriel's eyes widened in horror when he saw Lyra. But when he spotted Roger, he calmed down.

"I came to save you." said Lyra. But Asriel did not seem to care. His rooms were very comfortable – it didn't appear he was a prisoner at all.

"What is Dust?" Lyra asked.

"Dust is what terrifies your mother and her colleagues," said Asriel. "They missed what was happening when they cut the bond linking children and their dæmons. A burst of tremendous energy, and they just didn't see it…"

Soon, Lyra and Roger went to sleep. But when she awoke, Roger was gone. Her father and his equipment had vanished, too. She called for Iorek.

"We've got to stop Asriel!" cried Lyra.

"The alethiometer says he'll hurt Roger!"

Lyra jumped up on to Iorek's back, and they pounded across sheets of ice towards the North Pole and Asriel. But a deep valley lay ahead – a thin, narrow bridge of ice reached across the gap.

"It won't hold you," Lyra told the Ice Bear.

"I'll have to go alone," she decided. Iorek knew that his brave young friend was right.

"Goodbye, Lyra Silvertongue," he said sadly.

Lyra wiped the tears from her eyes. Then she and Pan crossed the bridge. Suddenly they were dazzled by a vast sheet of shimmering colour – green and red and blue – that stretched across the sky. And behind it was the ghostly shape of a huge city. Asriel was making sure his equipment was ready. Stelmaria, his snow-leopard dæmon, clutched Roger's dæmon in her mouth.

"Let her go!" cried Roger. "Lyra, make him stop!"

But before Lyra could do anything, Asriel had flipped a switch. Roger's dæmon exploded! Then a great flash of bright energy shot from Roger into the air. The light tore the sky open, creating a gateway to another world – but Roger was gone.

"What have you done?" said a furious voice.

Mrs Coulter had appeared, as if from nowhere.

"Will you come with me to the other world, Marisa?" Asriel asked.

"I can't," said Mrs Coulter. "I daren't."

"How could you do that to Roger?" Lyra cried.

"You have no idea what's at stake," said Asriel simply. "One child doesn't matter."

He marched into the swirling sky – and was gone.

Suddenly, the icy ground split open, separating Lyra and Mrs Coulter. Within seconds, Mrs Coulter disappeared from view. Then Lyra had a sudden thought. Her father had told her that there were billions of other worlds. And that meant there could be a world where Roger was alive!

Lyra saw tiny pinpricks of light move towards the alethiometer. Then the needle began to spin. "It's Dust!" Lyra cried. "Dust makes the needle move! It says that I know the way." Lyra looked up at the shimmering hole in the sky.

Quickly, she made a decision.

"We'll follow the Dust and we'll learn about it – and we'll bring Roger back!"

She stood up, took a deep breath and closed her eyes. Then she and Pan walked out of their world, into whatever lay beyond.